FARM BOY'S YEAR

FARM BOY'S YEAR

by David McPhail

Atheneum 1992 New York

Maxwell Macmillan Canada
Toronto
Maxwell Macmillan International
New York   Oxford   Singapore   Sydney

Library of Congress Cataloging-in-Publication Data

McPhail, David M. Farm boy's year/written and illustrated by David McPhail. — 1st ed. p.   cm. Summary: Diary entries and illustrations evoke a boy's life on a New England farm in the 1800s. ISBN 0–689–31679–8. [1. Farm life — Fiction. 2. New England — Fiction. 3. Diaries — Fiction.] I. Title. PZ7.M2427Fap   1992   [E] — dc20   91–4982

For Albert, and all the Lambs
D. M.

I grew up along a section of the New England coast where the sand dunes rise up to protect the fragile, fertile marsh from the relentless pounding of the ocean waves.

Farther inland, beyond the marsh, rise the low hills where the first settlers established farms, many of which still provide vegetables and milk products to the residents of the nearby towns.

When I pass one of these farms, I sometimes wonder what it was like to live there a century ago—before airplanes, automobiles, and televisions.

Here is how I imagine it might have been, through the eyes of a twelve-year-old boy.

David McPhail

January

January 9

    Went sledding with Joey Parsons on March's Hill. The new sled I got for Christmas was the fastest one there.

    From the top of the hill, I could see Father and Uncle John cutting blocks of ice at Quill's Pond.

    The ice will be packed in sawdust in the barn next to the pond. Then, next summer, Uncle John will sell it to the townsfolk, a chunk at a time.

February

February 12

    Blizzard is in its second day. The snow is already up to the kitchen window. No school.

    Helped Mother bake bread in the morning.

    Worked alongside Father at the forge till evening. I made a scythe blade all by myself. Can't wait to try it out.

March

March 4

    Up before dawn to make maple syrup. Drove the team while Father collected the sap.

    We built a fire in the sugarhouse under the evaporator, and when it boiled down, we drained off the syrup.

    It takes a lot of time, a lot of wood, and a lot of sap to make a gallon of syrup. We made twenty-three gallons today.

April

April 1

    The first warm day of spring. Skipped school and went fishing with Joey. Caught a boatload of flounder.

    Mother wasn't pleased that I skipped school, but she sure liked having the flounder.

    She told me to go around and invite the neighbors for a fish fry, then come back and clean the fish.

    By the time I finished cleaning them, I wasn't very hungry.

May

May 14

Every year on this date, the cows get put out to pasture. When I ask why *this* date, everybody has a different answer.

Fred, the hired man, says that the grass isn't ready till now.

Father says that the cows' stomachs aren't ready for green grass before today.

Mother says they're both wrong. She says it's just the way it's always been and nobody's ever asked why.

I think she's right. She usually is.

June

June 17

    Last day of school. Thought it would never come.

    Such a beautiful day that Miss Gould let us out early. I think she's happy that school's out for the summer too.

    Joey Parsons and I plan to do nothing but swim and fish. I think my father has other ideas, though. At breakfast I heard him mention that the sugar snap peas are almost ready to pick.

July

July 3

Hayed again today. Been haying all week, but this is the last load. The barn is just about full.

I made a drum out of an old grain sieve, and I'm going to march with it tomorrow in the Fourth of July parade.

August

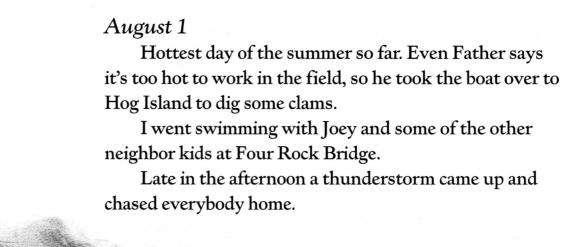

August 1

Hottest day of the summer so far. Even Father says it's too hot to work in the field, so he took the boat over to Hog Island to dig some clams.

I went swimming with Joey and some of the other neighbor kids at Four Rock Bridge.

Late in the afternoon a thunderstorm came up and chased everybody home.

September

September 13

Today was my birthday. I got a brand-new pocketknife. Mother showed me how to sharpen it. Then I whittled a new latch for the henhouse.

Tomorrow I'm going to start carving some decoys to set out when I go hunting. Father says this year it's up to me to put a goose on the table for Thanksgiving.

October

October 19

Picked apples today. It was warm for October. Mother made a half dozen pies (can't wait for supper).

Father took a cart full of the apples to the barn to press them into cider. I helped. He says I drink it almost as fast as he makes it.

It tastes good now, and it will taste good next summer when we're haying.

November

November 24

    Went hunting on the marsh. Brought home a fat goose for Thanksgiving dinner.

    Mom says I must be a good shot. Truth is, I couldn't miss. There must have been a million of them.

    All my relatives are coming for Thanksgiving dinner. Aunts, uncles, cousins, and grandparents—twenty-one in all. Can't wait!

December

December 21

    Father and I looked all over the farm for a suitable
Christmas tree but couldn't find one. Then I remembered
where I'd seen one last fall when I was hunting quail—
in the little woods on the far side of the cornfield.

    It was just getting dark when I found it. Everybody
says it's the best tree we ever had.

December 31

    When I checked the thermometer on my way upstairs to bed, the glass read seventeen below. It feels almost that cold in my room.

    The moon is so bright I don't need a candle to write this.

    I can hear the ice on the pond shifting, and the frozen trees crack like gunshots.

    As I climb into my cold bed, I think ahead to summer— to haying in the hot sun. Soon I'll pull the quilt up over my ears and drift off to sleep.